Sharon, Lois & Bram's
Peanut Butter and Jelly

story by Randi Hampson
illustrated by Qin Leng

tundra

To Jennifer who is with us every step of the way and adds so much! — S, B & R

To my father, Joe, who is the reason I LOVE peanut butter and jelly! I know this would have made him smile. — R

Text copyright © 2023 by Randi Hampson, Sharon Hampson, Lois Lilienstein and Bram Morrison
Illustrations copyright © 2023 by Qin Leng

Tundra Books, an imprint of Tundra Book Group, a division of Penguin Random House of Canada Limited

Library and Archives Canada Cataloguing in Publication

Title: Peanut butter and jelly / Sharon Hampson, Lois Lilienstein and Bram Morrison ; illustrated by Qin Leng.
Names: Hampson, Sharon, author. | Lilienstein, Lois, author. | Morrison, Bram, author. | Leng, Qin, illustrator.
Identifiers: Canadiana (print) 20210353740 | Canadiana (ebook) 20210353953 | ISBN 9780735271104 (hardcover) | ISBN 9780735271111 (EPUB)
Subjects: LCGFT: Picture books.
Classification: LCC PS8615.A5456 P43 2023 | DDC jC813/.6-dc23

Edited by Elizabeth Kribs
Designed by John Martz and Sophie Paas-Lang
The artwork in this book was created with ink and watercolor.
The text was set in Burbank Small.

Printed in China

www.penguinrandomhouse.ca

1 2 3 4 5   27 26 25 24 23

Penguin
Random House
tundra | TUNDRA BOOKS

One of our favorite things to sing about is food, and this delicious song is an inclusive, fun, safe, allergy-free way to enjoy a peanut butter sandwich. A fifth-grade class taught Bram the "Peanut Butter and Jelly" song, and we all liked it so much that we made it the first song of our second album, *Smorgasbord*. It has been a huge hit with our fans ever since. At our concerts, audiences young and old alike stand up and sing and dance as a group. We do the actions together: digging, picking, crushing, spreading, biting, munching and swallowing.

Clap and sing and do the actions with your family and friends! It can be as much fun as sharing a delicious lunch together – Mmm mmm mmmm!

Photo: David Cooper

If your tummy is agrumbly
and you don't know what to eat,

Come join us in the kitchen as
we make a tasty treat.

Peanut,
peanut butter,
JELLY!

Peanut,
peanut butter,
JELLY!

Roll up your sleeves and wash your hands
so we can prepare.

We baked ourselves a loaf of bread –
there's plenty here to share.

Peanut,
peanut butter,
JELLY!
Peanut,
peanut butter,
JELLY!

We thought the jars were waiting
for us right there on the shelves,

But, NO, it seems we need to
make the toppings all ourselves.

Peanut, peanut butter, JELLY!

Peanut, peanut butter, JELLY!

We all are getting hungry and
don't want a tummy ache,

So come on an adventure
because it's time to make . . .

Peanut,
peanut butter,
JELLY!

Peanut,
peanut butter,
JELLY!

First you dig the peanuts and
you dig 'em,
you dig 'em,

Then
you crush 'em,
you crush 'em,

you crush 'em
crush 'em
crush 'em.

Then
 you spread 'em,
  you spread 'em,

you spread 'em
spread 'em
spread 'em.

Peanut,
peanut butter,
JELLY!

Peanut,
peanut butter,
JELLY!

Next you pick the berries and you pick 'em,
you pick 'em,

you pick 'em   pick 'em   pick 'em.

Then
you crush 'em,
you crush 'em,

you crush 'em
crush 'em
crush 'em.

Then
    you spread 'em,
        you spread 'em,

you spread 'em
spread 'em
spread 'em.

Peanut,
peanut butter,
JELLY!

Peanut,
peanut butter,
JELLY!

Then you bite the sandwich and
you bite it,
you bite it,

you bite it
bite it
bite it.

Then
you munch it,
you munch it,

you munch it
munch it
munch it.

Then
you swallow, GULP
you swallow, GULP

you swallow
swallow
swallow . . .

Mmmmmmm mmmmmmmmm mmmmm mmmm mmmmmmmm mmmmmmmmmm mmmmmmm mmmmmm mmmmm

Tomorrow we'll be back again and no one will complain,

Because we always clean the kitchen so that no more crumbs remain!

If you like this sandwich, there are things that you can do
To make a different tasty treat with ingredients that are new.

Try almond or soybean or pecan butter spread
With raspberry or strawberry jam upon your bread.

On some challah or on gluten-free or yummy multigrain
With some honey or banana or eat your bread just plain!

SHARON HAMPSON, the late **LOIS LILIENSTEIN** (d. 2015) and **BRAM MORRISON** are some of Canada's most famous children's performers, with fans across North America and around the world. The trio, known simply as Sharon, Lois & Bram, formed in Toronto in 1978 and went on to create two top-rated children's television shows, *The Elephant Show* and *Skinnamarink TV*, and twenty-one full-length albums. Their songs feature silly animals, stories about friendship and themes of love. If you look closely, you can see characters from some of Sharon, Lois and Bram's most popular songs in this book! After Bram's retirement from touring in 2019 and with his enthusiastic support, Sharon and her daughter, **RANDI HAMPSON**, continue to entertain children and share their message of love through their music. You can find out more on www.sharonloisandbram.com or by following Sharon, Bram and Randi on social media @sharonloisbram.

QIN LENG is an award-winning designer and illustrator known for her children's book illustrations. Qin has illustrated numerous picture books, including *Sharon, Lois & Bram's Skinnamarink* and *One Elephant Went Out to Play*, as well as *Over the Shop*, *A Day for Sandcastles* and *A Family Is a Family Is a Family*. She lives in Toronto with her husband and son. Please visit www.qinillustrations.com.

Look out for these other books from Sharon, Lois & Bram!